SEVENTH CIRCLE PRESS
P.O. Box 150107
Kew Gardens, NY 11415-0107
www.seventhcirclepress.com

Library of Congress Control Number: 2008923160

First Seventh Circle Press printing: April 2008

Printed in the United States of America

Darling Wendy

and other stories

MELISSA CRANDALL

For Pam Hohmann and David Jessup

Always there

ACKNOWLEDGMENTS

Thank you to these folks for help along the way:

Ed Everett, Síofra Shaman Skye, N.M. Kelby, Karen Heuler, Glenda Baker and Nina Spaziani ("*You da man!*").

"Darling Wendy" originally appeared in *New England Writers' Network Magazine* as winner of their 2002 Short Story Contest.

"Moonwalk" and "Transformation" originally appeared in *5.5BW: Poems and Stories*, published by Seventh Circle Press (2007).

TABLE OF CONTENTS

And To All a Good Night

The first snowfall of the year is still inside you somewhere.

-- *Barbara Crafton*
"First Flakes: Just One of Those Things"

They gather in private homes and public venues; come together in bars and restaurants, school gymnasiums and auditoriums. In stadiums and on playing fields, in theatres and drive-ins, in hospitals and sanitariums, the population of the Earth – in its entirety – queues, jostles, stands, sits and hangs from any location that will let them connect to the virtual channel that is available only once a year. Like passengers aboard an aircraft, they strap in and wait. One child, unwilling to have a beloved pet miss the occasion, plugs in his dog. The animal doesn't give a damn, and promptly falls asleep.

Nella doesn't know where she is. Doesn't know *who* she is most of the time, come to that. Her life – once a riot of vibrant hues like the palette of an artist gone mad – is now featureless, and as grey as an old mattress. This is not because she is blind, but because she is old. Ancient. The years have pulled her attention inward, away from the present and into a past where sporadic bursts of illumination color a bleak and barren landscape.

1

All over the world, people settle in with hearts thumping, and take deep breaths in a futile attempt to stem the rising tide of anticipation that threatens to burst them apart. Drinks and food are put aside with restless hands. Fingers twine around one another, loosen, twine again. Feet jiggle a nervous dance. Someone sighs and shifts in her seat, unable to get comfortable. Another coughs and clears his throat. The petulant cry of a child sounds and is hushed. Neighbors share a smile and exhaustion drops from the tired creases of their eyes like confetti.

As a commodity, Nella sells herself. Her caretakers hardly need the slew of ad men eager to promote her. (The word *exploit* is never used.) Once word got out... *BLAM!* She took off like the rockets that once journeyed into space, reaching her destination every time and delivering her payload without mishap.

Unlike those ships, she can return home unscathed, to be reused again.

Indefinitely.

And, oh, but don't companies pay big to advertise in her time-slot! There are no commercials during transmission. Nothing is allowed to interrupt the flow. But the crowd must be entertained – and its greed stimulated – before the main attraction. Afterward, emotionally spent, they'll need something to keep high the nostalgic wave, something they can grasp with paycheck and credit card, ephemera to fool themselves into believing that what they just experienced is *real* beyond the time it takes to get home...where they fall into bed and wake in the morning aching with memory.

And if the sale of antidepressants rises during the holidays, what of it? The drug companies are some of her biggest sponsors.

In upstate New York, at the center of a ghost town that was once Victory Mills, is a scratched headstone atop a short plinth. It stands ignored but for the occasional pilgrim whose fingers brush its surface as they bend to read the scarred and faded inscription:

The last snowfall on Earth
occurred at this location,
December 13, 2007.
1.3"

"Nella? Wake up, old girl." The technician, one in a long line of faceless entities whose job it is to care for her, bends to check the readouts, turns a lever, pushes a button, and makes slight adjustments to the formula that runs through the tubes that connect her frail body to the machine. "Come on, honey. Wake up."

She stirs in her chair, rubbing her cheek against the bolster that keeps her head from flopping sideways. Her eyes open. The rheumy gaze floats for a moment, wandering, and then fastens on the young man with surprising clarity. She smiles at him. "Good morning, Daddy!"

"Good morning. We have a busy day ahead of us." In his few years with her, he's been her husband Joseph, her son Charlie, her best friend Lillian. Now it's Daddy. It makes no difference to him. He isn't paid to be a person, or to engage her in idle chatter.

Excited, she struggles to sit up, hands moving feebly on emaciated wrists. "What's happened?"

"Why, it snowed last night, that's what happened." He's mouthed these words or others like them so often that he no longer needs the script, but can improvise with ease. Peeling contact paper off round leads joined by wireless connection to the machine, he presses them to her temples, over her heart, between her eyebrows, and inserts a long, slender needle into a hollow receptacle implanted at the base of her skull. "You remember snow, don't you, Nella?"

She laughs. "Of course I remember, Daddy! It snows every year on my birthday!"

4

"And today's your birthday, my clever girl."
It's not, but she can't know that and he couldn't
care less. As drugs and electrical stimulus engage,
washing through her, he leans close. "Remember
snow, Nella," he whispers in her ear. "Remember
snow. Remember..."

Is that sound the memory of wind through
the bare branches of trees that no longer exist, or is
it the collective sigh of numberless throats?

Her warm breath clouds the air as, chuffing
like a locomotive, she climbs the long slope of the
hill. On the summit, nine year old Nella closes her
eyes, lifts her face to the cloudy sky, and draws a
deep breath through her nose, smelling snow on
the wind. It's a hard scent. Metallic. Almost
medicinal. Pine resin, alcohol, iron and wet wool.
Clean and cold. She can smell it coming long
before the storm arrives, but her favorite part is
when the wind kicks up, skirling the rag ends of
dead grass and withered leaves around her boots.
The chill deepens, gnawing her cheeks, worrying
the tips of her fingers, and crisping the hair in her
nose.

Across the world, heads lift. Nostrils flare,
seeking the elusive green scent of turpentine and
the blue smell of cold.

She stares into the sky, eyes watering, afraid to blink for fear of missing it. The first flake. When she finds it, there's nothing that could drag away her gaze. She watches it with the avid longing of a hungry man eyeing an approaching meal.

It's a lone emissary, sent on recognizance, shy and reticent. *Friend or foe?* it wonders, dancing before her eyes, spinning arabesques on the wind.

"Friend!" Nella whoops and whirls in circles, arms raised and thrown wide to encompass the sky and embrace the storm. As if that word were all the magic it takes, the sacred key, the code for which they wait, the clouds shake like wet dogs and surrender their cargo.

On land and sea, atop mountains and deep under ground, voices blend and lift in a communal cry of awe and joy. Laughter rings like the sound of rare bells. Tears of happiness course cheeks gone dry and dusty. Seeking hands reach, beseeching, to feel the burning bite of cold flakes melt against their skin.

Snow catches on the wool of her mittens, pure white on blood red, and holds a moment…two…before it melts into beads that reflect the world upside down.

Clouds dampen the light, monochrome the sky. Against them, the flakes appear a darker shade of grey until they land and turn white on white on white. As the sun breaks through, the snow glimmers like enchantment, like a million fairy lights, tiny sparks of magenta and amethyst, goldenrod and sea green. When it melts and refreezes, leaving a crust so thick it holds her weight, sunlight screams off of it in an arc of such brilliance that Nella must squint against the glare and lift a hand to shield her eyes. Dusk brings a blue edge to the drifts, indigo and sapphire and lapis.

Everywhere, hands turn palm up and then down, admiring the lattice of flakes that perch upon the fuzz of red wool. Eyes squint and water against a dazzling brilliance and then watch, at day's end, as the setting sun bleeds color across the snow and sends shadows running to bruise the ground to the color of plums.

Nella listens to the voice of the snow as it falls. In the air, it's a faint whisper, flake against flake, like insect legs on glass or the murmur of distant waves against sand. On Autumn's discarded leaves, curled like dead hands, the sound is sharper, crackling, pocking the crisp vegetation like tiny stones. At night, grasped tight and squeeze by cold, it squeaks and squeals in the tiny wailing voice of wood rubbing together.

Mounding up, piling deep and deeper still, the sound grows abyssal, almost beyond hearing, like the low, ponderous notes of whale song.

Ears strain to catch the sound. Some of those listening feel it in their chest, vibrating behind their breast bone, deep within their hearts. Some feel it slide across their tongues, thick and viscous, making their teeth ache with its sweetness. For others, it sinks into the skin, into their cells, until their entire body trembles and peals with sound.

Walking, Nella stamps her feet, kicking high in front with her toes and then behind with her heels, pretending to be a horse. The snow weighs heavily in the boot treads, dragging at her legs as she trudges through drifts that are hip-deep on her child's frame. Damp cold penetrates her snow pants and the shoulders of her coat. There are clots of snow down the wrist of each mitten, caught in the folds of her scarf, and inside her boots, but she won't be called in. Loathe to surrender winter for the lure of the fireside's warmth, she ignores the distant sound of her mother's cry, licks chapped lips, making them sting, and rubs the raw end of her nose. Snow clings to her eyelashes like a dusting of flour, and lands on her wind-reddened cheeks with a tiny sting of cold that almost burns in the instant before it melts and runs against her skin.

Mouth open, tongue extended, Winter's child drinks it in, tasting metal and earth, clouds and stars, dreams and wishes. Arms wide, she spins round and round until, dizzy, she falls onto her back, laughing, and flaps her arms and legs to make an angel.

She lays in the drift, eyes closed against the fall of icy stars, heart thundering with delight. Better than the feel of snow, better than all the sights and smells, sounds and tastes, is what it does inside of her, warming her soul with a wave of joy too immense to be contained by the lowly vessel of her body. The rapture grows, pushing at her skin from the inside, and expands like a star going nova.

"Nella?"

Memories calve like glacial ice and run like melted snow. Across the world, in every land, people jerk in protest, thrust out of their dreams with the rude awakening of nightmare. They blink in confusion, turning questioning eyes to each other, to the monitors which show only grey. Some hug themselves, or reach for loved ones. A few begin to cry. The small, frightened sound of sorrow grows, widens, and broadens into a storm.

"Shit! Nella, goddammit!"

There is no response, no lurch and jerk, no grasping of hands, no death rattle. The monitor simply flat-lines. The feeds – flawless and engaged – empty of their cocktail and become flaccid. The technician, useless, hovers, hands and mind limp, unable to move. Trained to deal with any mechanical eventuality, he has no idea what to do with a human life who has had enough.

He watches her...hesitant, unsure. A tear wells along the edge of a dead eye and perches, held in place by a fold of ancient skin. He looks at it, head tilting one way and then another, watching the play of color in the tiny drop of fluid. Then, reaching, he touches it, brings the damp finger to his mouth, and tastes cold.

Goodbye, Norma Jeane

He beat her to the cemetery, but she expected that. For as long as she'd known him, he was the methodical one – thoughtful in planning, slow to act, (except on the ball field; then, if you were wise, you'd grab your hat and hang on tight). She, on the other hand, was the dazzler – an electric spark, a carnival ride. She'd found it hard to walk sedately by his side. Even when she managed, there was always a lilt to her step, a jiggle that belied her enthusiasm for life. Fidgety as a kid in church, dragging him along behind her, she couldn't wait to run ahead and see what lay around the next corner. This time, he got there first, sliding into home ahead of her.

She hadn't gone to the funeral. Couldn't, really, and not just because his family had never liked her. The stuffy bunch would have had fits in more ways than one if she'd chosen his funeral as the time to make an appearance. The thought of the commotion that would have ensued – the media circus – teased a small, sadly wry smile from the corner of her mouth. The last thing she wanted to see was a reporter or a photographer.

A gentle wind tugged the short curls of her hair. She imagined it to be the touch of his fingers, trailing through strands that had decreased in value over time, silver now instead of platinum. He'd asked her to let it go back to its natural color – the auburn-touched brown of her youth – but she'd refused, liking the change. She complied, finally, when he was no longer around much to admire it.

Guilt poked her under the heart still. She shook it away with an impatient toss of her head.

Picking her careful way among the graves of Holy Cross Cemetery, she paused now and then to read a headstone, but mostly kept her eyes to the ground, watching her step. The cemetery was well-tended and flat; it looked nothing like the 300 acre potato farm it once had been, but she was 73 years old and needed to "keep careful," as her grandmother would have said. Her health was good. She was active – playing golf, riding her bicycle, walking the dog – and wanted it to stay that way. The last thing she needed was a twisted ankle or – heaven forbid! – a broken hip.

She glimpsed the gravesite in the near distance and paused to stare. She'd waited a long time to come here to pay her respects, longer than she'd intended or he deserved. Perhaps she'd been afraid of discovery, although there were blessed few left alive who'd recognize her now. Her reluctance certainly wasn't out of embarrassment. There was nothing left for either of them to be embarrassed about. The world had seen to that, throwing the hardest pitches it could. Always the better hitter, he stayed in the game until the end while she chose to strike out, play it safe and, with his help, retire from the field.

Her heart thumped like a memory of new love and she started forward, stepping carefully, her eyes now trained ahead on the black slab of rock that marked his eternal resting place. Even after all this time, the grave was heaped with flowers. She imagined that a lot of people came here, and wondered at her luck at finding him alone, all hers for a change.

Leaning forward, she brushed aside several bouquets in order to read the inscription. "Grace, Dignity, and Elegance Personified," she whispered, and smiled. "Well, that just about says it all, Joe."

Memories assailed her, rising in an unanticipated wave of feeling – of *passion* – that threatened to swamp her. So many moments shared – laughter, sorrow, rage – in the forty-five years of comfortable friendship that arose, phoenix-like, out of the ashes of their 18-month courtship and nine-month marriage. Their curse had been that they couldn't live with each other. Their blessing had been that they couldn't live *without* each other, either.

Tears shimmered on the surface of her eyes, making them look enormous, but she refused to blink and let them fall. He always hated it when she cried, so she would not do so now.

Moving slowly, drawing her coat around her, she lowered herself to the ground and settled with her legs tucked under her and to one side. Although she didn't realize it, the pose was one she'd often struck for photographers, albeit now lacking any flirtation. "Well, I'm here." Her voice was husky. She sniffed, dug a tissue out of her coat pocket, and swiped with irritation at her nose. "Bet you thought I'd never make it, huh?" The black stone was silent.

She looked away, gazing out over this land of the dead. Cranky and contrary as a toddler when it came to weather, this part of California was blessed with surprisingly mild springs. This day was cloudless, warm and dry, and she noted it with amusement. "Bet you'd rather be playing ball." Only the wind answered.

The words came in a rush, sudden and unexpected as illness. "Did I ever thank you properly, Joe? I can't remember. I hope I did. You were the truest friend I ever had. No matter how bad things got, no matter how bad *I* became, you were always there, always my knight in shining armor, riding to the rescue." One fist gently pounded her thigh and now, despite her promise to herself, the tears did fall, tracking the course of that still lovely face, running into the lines around her mouth and dripping off her chin to spot the caramel wool of her slacks.

As if it were yesterday, she remembered with vivid brightness when her world cracked and it all went tumbling down. Remembered the pain and fear, the booze and drugs, the rage and recrimination and the late-night phone call swearing that she wanted to die, *promising* that she'd kill herself this time, she'd really do it up right and be done, and the rest of the world could go to Hell!

There was a blank space in the memory, a time of blackness, and then he was there, coming in to find her curled tight as a fist in her bed, naked like the cheap whore everyone but he thought she was. He'd drawn a hot tub, gathered her up like a little girl, bathed her tired body, soothed her wasted mind, and promised her that if she wanted it all to go away – *really* wanted it – then he would make it so they could never find her.

The goddess died that night, sprawled nude across her bed as flashbulbs popped. Perhaps all those rumors about Joe and various high-powered Italian men were true after all. She hadn't asked. In the end, a woman who was simply a woman rose from that mattress, dressed, and took the hand of the only man she'd ever trusted. Taking nothing,

14

she let him lead her away, where she disappeared into life.

"It's over here! Dad, it's over here!"

Her head rose. Wind chapped the tears against her cheeks. There were people coming, a man with two young boys, one of them carrying a baseball bat, the other a glove. She saw the father notice her, try to make his sons wait, but they rushed forward, eager to pay homage to their hero. She understood.

Wiping trembling fingers against her face, she rose, teetered, caught her balance on the headstone, and gave it a pat. "See you around, Joe," she said softly and, as once before, vanished into the lengthening shadows.

Transformation

Gripping the steering wheel tight enough to punch circles of white over each knuckle, Kate Freeman slams her foot down on the brake. The battered pickup fishtails and comes to a rocking, jolting stop in the middle of the slushy back-country road. Breathing hard, black spots swarming across her vision, she scrabbles for the door handle, finds the window crank instead, and rolls the window down just in time.

Beside her on the bench seat, Hannibal whines an anxious question. Slinking into her lap, the border collie touches a cold nose to her cheek and, unfazed by the ripe stink of vomit, licks a warm track through her tears. Sobbing, Kate buries her face in the dog's ruff and hugs him. "I can't do this, Eric," she whispers. "I just can't." Hannibal's tail thumps a mournful tattoo against the upholstery as chill air, sharp with the turpentine bite of pine resin, touches a breezy finger to her cheek.

ଔ

They met by chance, burrowing through the stacks at a secondhand bookstore. Reaching for the same copy of Don Quixote, *their hands collided and their gazes met in a look of surprise. Eric maintained that he never understood what prompted him to invite her out for coffee. Burned by a nasty divorce and with two children grown and on their own, Eric was cautious around women and had decided that maybe middle age was a good time to be unencumbered by emotional attachments. He had no thoughts of becoming involved* with anyone, let alone a woman twenty years his junior. For her part, Kate was shocked to hear herself accept his invitation. Scarred as well by past relationships, she was even more wary.

What occurred, much to their mutual amazement, was that those two cups of coffee became a prelude to quick lunches crammed between the busyness of Eric's teaching schedule and Kate's veterinary clients. That, in turn, gradually developed into late-night phone calls, lingering take-out dinners, and long conversations over mid-priced wine and the Scrabble® board. What emerged over the course of the months that followed was a love grounded in solid friendship. Bitter experience had taught Kate not to believe any nonsense about soul mates, but in Eric she had proof that such magic did exist.

Married five years, they decided to jerk up their roots in northern California and move to western Alaska, Kate to run a clinic (an advertisement offering a veterinary practice for sale prompted the notion) and Eric to teach geology at the local schools.

Another five years saw them happy in their lives, content with their work and their new community, and still wildly in love. In their spare time they hiked the high country, spying on whatever wildlife chose to share itself. Eric loved the eagles best, but it was the caribou that won Kate's devotion, their solid presence reminding her of her husband.

Just when it was almost too perfect, when waking each morning caught Kate's breath with a swell of gratitude, Eric began to experience back pain.

℃ℨ

Kate drives into town with her gut churning. Work is the last thing she feels like doing, but she needs something to occupy the endless roll of hours. The eerie silence of the house peals like a clarion, the absence of Eric's voice echoing like a gunshot in the mountains. Television is a bore and movies are painful. Music brings no solace, and walking the trails she once climbed with Eric is unthinkable, even to scatter his ashes.

As she guides the truck along the little town's main street, pedestrians look up, smile, and wave. Kate returns their greetings with the gestures of an automaton, smiling the fake smile she's adopted over the past ten months. Parking the truck in its accustomed spot in front of the clinic, she stifles a groan.

Each store in the tiny downtown has a front porch with a gathering of mismatched, sway-seated chairs. On any given day, they are occupied almost exclusively by the elders of the community as they take the sun or pause to chat during their small bits of shopping. There are three such chairs in front of the clinic, and Kate's self-appointed guardian angels are in place: three old guffers with nothing better to do than chew over the past, gossip about their neighbors, and keep an eye on her.

Kate knows they mean well, and she's never minded until now, seeing their interest as less an expression of nosiness than of proof that she and Eric have earned their place in the community family. Understanding all this, Kate still wants to tell them to shove their curiosity straight up their octogenarian butts. Instead, she cuts the ignition, gets out of the truck, and lets Hannibal bound past her to greet the men.

"G'mornin,' Doc!" Jacob Holloway, age-spotted and turkey-wattled, lifts a shaky hand off the head of his cane to pet the dog. The undisputed leader of the triumvirate, he has the middle chair as place of honor. Flanking him, skinny Ed Nightnose (who resembles nothing so much as a strip of beef jerky) and zeppelin-esque Andy Morris nod their sage greetings.

"Good morning, gentlemen. Lovely day."

Andy, who is happiest when being contrary and does his utmost to be happy all the time, shakes his head. "S'posed to snow later."

Hidden from sight inside Kate's jacket pocket, one middle finger thrusts in his direction. "Well, I guess it does that in Alaska." Unlocking the clinic door, she whistles Hannibal to her and escapes inside, but not before hearing Ed decree in the tones of a judge handing down a verdict, "She looks like shit."

☙

She was wrapping Christmas presents to send to friends and family in the lower forty-eight when Eric came through the door. Still stung by his refusal to let her accompany him on the long trip to the doctor's office to learn the results of tests taken the week before, she watched in silence as he petted Hannibal and then stamped the snow from his boots, toed them off onto the mat, shrugged out of his coat, stuffed his gloves into the pockets before hanging it behind the door, and unwound the long red scarf she'd bought for him because it made him look like Bob Cratchitt. Did she imagine it, or was he moving more slowly than his pain ordinarily allowed, with a pace measured so as not to waste energy?

She rose then, feeling small and mean-spirited for her silence, and padded over in stocking feet to greet him, going up on her toes to hug him, her warm cheek against his cold one. He held her a moment, face buried in that spot he loved where her neck joined her shoulder, breathing in her scent through the warm flannel of her shirt. "Trip go okay?" she finally asked.

He nodded, brushing her hair with his nose. "It's started snowing again."

She glanced out the big front window. Looked like they'd have a white Thanksgiving next week. This year the celebration was at their place, with friends from town invited in for the festivities. "You want something warm to drink? Tea? Cocoa? Coffee?"

He nodded again. "Cocoa'd be great." He seemed loathe to let her go, so Kate hooked his little finger with hers and drew him along behind her into the galley-style kitchen, trying all the while to ignore the patter of panicky feet inside her stomach.

Eric hovered behind her like a moth at a candle flame while she measured the milk, heated it in a saucepan, whisked in the cocoa. As a treat, she added a dollop of whipped cream to each cup. (Her brother Ken referred to the pressurized stuff as 'whip-ass in a can.' Suddenly, with a ferocity as frightening as it was unexpected, she wanted him with her.)

Before she could ask where he'd like to sit – by the fire or in the breakfast nook where they could watch the snow – Eric put his arms around her from behind and squeezed her tight. In that

20

moment Kate knew the worst had happened. She closed her eyes against a rush of tears as he said, "Honey, I have some bad news."

൪

Inside the clinic, Kate forces herself through the morning routine. Flick on the lights, crank open the window blinds halfway, pick up the mail off the floor. Three checks, two advertisements and – will wonders never cease? – no bills. There are three phone messages -- Sammy Tem's goat is better thank you very much, Mrs. Mondeville needs more hairball remedy for Gregory, and six-year-old Louie Sweetcreek's ancient budgie has finally shuffled off his mortal coil, so please come to the funeral tomorrow at nine ayem. The appointment book shows no morning surgeries and just a couple of routine visits in the afternoon. Good. Unless there's an emergency, she has plenty of time to compose an advertisement similar to the one that brought her here.

A part of her feels traitorous for selling the practice. The move to Alaska was a dream come true, but the dream died with Eric. She is so tired of going on alone. She has no intention of killing herself – her depression isn't so severe and she often feels guilty about that as well – but this morning's vomiting proves that she doesn't have what it takes to stay in Alaska without him. She has no idea where she'll go, but her childhood home in Massachusetts looks good, at least for now. Ken and his family live in the area, so she'll have moral support. Maybe settling someplace where Eric never lived will help her move on. As things stand, waking each morning to a house filled with his spirit, surrounded by his things and mementoes of

21

their shared life, in a land he fervently loved, is doing her no good at all.

ભ

Waking that night, her face against the damp pillow, Kate realized that Eric's side of the bed was empty. Shivering from more than cold, she got up, pulled on a thick robe, and went downstairs with Hannibal at her heels.

She didn't see him at first, for the living room was dark, the fire banked, and she didn't think to look out onto the porch. But there he was – pajama'd and parka'd, wearing the silly doggy slippers his grandkids had sent him from Minnesota – standing at the railing, watching it snow, drinking wine.

She paused, debating whether to intrude on his solitude. She watched the snow settle on his hair, white on white, watched him lift his eyes to the shifting storm, blink snow from his pale lashes, smile, laugh, press one hand into the small of his back and, with the other, raise his glass in a salute to…what? The storm? Nature? The universe? God and the great joke he'd played on them?

Advanced pancreatic cancer.

Shit.

Eric turned then, saw her standing in the shadows at the foot of the stairs, and waved her out onto the porch to revel in the storm. Of course she went. Closing the slider behind her, Kate stepped into the warmth of her husband's embrace, sipped the wine he offered, and was silently grateful for the snow melting on her face, disguising her tears.

ભ

22

Why Eric's death didn't kill her, Kate doesn't know. The passage of ten months has done nothing to ease her agony. Mornings no longer hold the joy of waking to his kiss. Now the sun greets her with the memory of waking on the couch, his hospital bed no more than two feet away, placed near the windows so Eric can see the mountains. From the television comes the distant noise of celebration as revelers cheer in the New Year, and she knows, even before she sits up, that he's slipped away without letting her watch him go. Thus abandoned, she has an Eric-shaped hole in her soul that cannot be filled.

Just before noon, in the midst of breaking down cardboard boxes from the local bar to take home for packing, the bell over the door jangles. Hannibal looks up from his spot beneath the desk, then barks a greeting and jets, all wiggle-assed, into the arms of Chris Crowtree. A neighbor on the mountain, Chris runs the local radio station and, with his wife Chloe, parents a hoard of the most beautiful bronze-skinned children Kate has ever seen. "Buy the doctor some lunch?" he asks with a charming grin.

"No, thanks."

He holds up two brown sacks from the deli (*Wagner's* is emblazoned on the side in red) and waggles them just out of reach of the jumping dog. "Too late, already done. Reuben on toasted rye with extra Russian dressing, a dill pickle, and a cold root beer."

Kate takes a slow, measured breath – she really doesn't want to go off on this man; he's been a good friend through it all – and tries to ignore the

23

red crescents of pain her fingernails carve into the palms of her hands. "*No,* Chris. Thank you."

His smile fades. "You gotta eat, Kate."

"I know what I gotta do, Chris, and I'm doing it," she says without explanation. "I appreciate your concern, but I don't need you mothering me."

"I'm not – "

"To hell you aren't!" Hannibal's ears droop at the anger in her voice. She can almost hear the last straw break as the fury finally breeches the careful façade of grieving-but-slowly-healing widow she's maintained all these months. "*Everyone's* got their nose in my life!"

Chris doesn't take offense. "You're our friend, Kate," he says softly. "We care about you. We just want to make sure you're okay."

"Well, I'm not okay. Maybe you can announce it on the radio." She throws her arms wide, not caring how ridiculous she appears. "Doctor Freeman is not fucking okay! How's that sound?" Snatching up an armload of flattened boxes, she storms past him, wrenches open the door, stomps down the porch steps, and flings the cardboard into the truck bed.

"Holy shit," said Ed Nightnose. "What do you make of that?"

Kate spins around, ready to tell him *precisely* what he can make of it, and realizes that he isn't talking about her. He's not even looking at her.

Andy's prediction of snow has borne fruit. A skirl of flakes – too heavy to be called flurries, too light yet to be a genuine storm – dances in the air, swirling and eddying in all directions. In the middle of the street, not more than twelve feet away, like a king heralded by the snow, stands a bull caribou.

24

The animal is a prime specimen, five feet tall at the shoulder, probably weighing close to four hundred pounds. The long, backswept antlers are branched, slightly flattened at the tip, with well-developed brow tines. His coat is clove brown, the neck and rump white, and the long hairs move as the rising wind brings Kate the musk of deep forests and wind-scoured winter plains.

And something else.

Hannibal barks, not a sharp note of warning, but a joyful yip of recognition. Neatly eluding Chris's grasp, the dog leaps down the steps and dashes for the beast.

"Hannibal, no!" Hands to her face, Kate watches in horror for the moment when the only other creature she loves is trampled to death beneath those broad, concave hooves. Instead, the dog bounds in the snow, dancing around the enormous animal with obvious joy. Rump in the air, he play-bows, tail waving with merry abandon. Bouncing forward, he rubs against the caribou's legs like a cat, then sits as if on command and waits for the animal to bend its great head and touch noses.

"You ever see a caribou around here?"

"Hell, I never saw anything like this in my life."

Kate doesn't know who spoke, but a quick glance at the men is enough to tell her they see only the dog and caribou, and not what she sees. They don't see the snow coalesce and swirl like mist, nor watch the caribou's form fade into pale shadow, its eyes change from black to blue as something – someone – steps out of its shape like an actor discarding a costume.

Afraid to blink, terrified to even breathe for fear of breaking whatever magic is occurring, Kate moves forward to meet her husband. Her knees buckle and Eric catches her by the arms. His hands are warm and *there* and strong, holding her. Shaking, Kate lifts her hands to trace the contours of his face – the prow nose, heavily lidded Nordic eyes, full mouth, and ragged mop of white hair, all of it so much beloved. Only when she's certain does she pull him close and breathe deeply, finally acknowledging what she'd smelled on the wind. Not the odor of wild animal or the sick stink of Eric near death, but the pungent scent that is all him, only him.

Neither speaks and how long they stand there, Kate can't say. All at once, there seems to be all the time in the universe and too little. Later, her audience will maintain that she communed with the beast for just a few seconds, just long enough to touch its coat. But for Kate, she is gifted with ages before her husband, her soul mate, releases her and resumes his new life.

Blinking back into what passes for reality in the rest of the world, Kate feels hot, moist breath on her face. The caribou snuffles her ear, lays its chin into the hollow where her neck joins her shoulder, then snorts, turns, and moves off at a mile-devouring trot straight down the street. At the corner, it pauses to utter a low, measured note, like the lifesaving cry of a lighthouse. The wind whips a heavy gust of snow around it and when it clears, the animal is gone.

"Kate?" Chris's voice seems to come from a long way off. It takes her a moment to acknowledge the hand on her arm. "Are you all right?"

It's difficult to focus on him with Eric's image still before her eyes. "I'm fine." Blinking hard, she wipes her eyes.

"I never saw anything like that! It came right up to you!"

A grin breaks over Kate's face. For the first time in months, the sheer joy of living throbs in her like a pulse. "Why don't we have those sandwiches, Chris? All of a sudden, I'm hungry." Laughter breaks free as something inside cracks open and slides away. Tonight, storm or not, she will climb a short distance up the mountain, scatter what remains of Eric's former life, and begin again.

Author's Note

A brief explanation is required for this next story. The original *Dreams on Racks* was penned by my long-time friend David Jessup. Among his many incarnations, Dave was the first student archivist for the Rod Serling Collection at Ithaca College, and wrote *Dreams on Racks* as an homage to Mr. Serling. (And if you don't know who Rod Serling was, go rent the original episodes of *Twilight Zone* and prepare to be blown away.)

Dave endeavored to sell the piece several times (most notably to the now-defunct *Twilight Zone Magazine*), without success and eventually filed it away for good. One day, in response to my saying how much I liked it, he dug it out, tossed it into my lap, and said, "If you can make something of it, get it sold finally, go for it!" The story languished in my files. I'd play with it, make some notes, toy with an idea or two, and put it away again. It didn't want to come together. And then, one day... it did, and the result is here.

In honor of Dave's original intent, this story should still be considered an homage to Rod Serling. But it's also an homage to almost 30 years of friendship.

Thanks, Davey.

Dreams on Racks

for Dave Jessup

There's better than seventy years' worth of film in the vaults of the U.S. Library of Congress, Department of Copyright, Motion Picture Division. Miles of people's imaginations neatly racked, sitting in perpetual twilight. All those dreams that people sweated over, sometimes died for – now shelved and forgotten by those who equate good filmmaking with flashy special effects, acres of cleavage, and monosyllabic dialogue.

I love every rack of it, every canister and hibernating vision. Films have been my passion for more than fifty years and I'm talking good films here, those with staying power, films created with thought and craft and ardor, not the garbage crunched out today just to turn a buck. Coming to work here was the attainment of a dream. To care for these films, to ensure their protection from the depredations of time, is an honor I take very seriously.

Which is why, being the sort of chronic nut-case I am, I stayed past quitting time and got nailed by my boss when he flipped a request chit into my basket. "What's that?"

"Last minute priority rush."

"Why me?"

"Because everyone with a lick of sense has gone home, Andy, and you have no life."

"I have a life!"

He made an obnoxious show of checking his watch against the wall clock, then gave me a slow once-over, taking in my sneakers, worn chinos, and denim shirt. "What are your plans for this Friday evening, Cinderella?"

I shrugged, annoyed at myself for feeling self-conscious. "Pick up some Chinese take-out, have a beer or two, put on some Goodman tunes, maybe catch a –"

"A what? Old *Star Trek* rerun? What about a date, companionship... *amore*?" He said the last like a bad actor in a third-rate Italian film, and then made a face. "Like I said, no life."

"Just because my life doesn't measure up to what *you* think it should be doesn't mean –"

"Yes, it does." He cut me off with a head shake and a sharky smile. "They want the flick first thing Monday morning, so make sure it's there by to-effin-night, okay? Make me look good." He had the nerve to wink as he turned to leave.

"Wait a minute!" My voice caught him and he swung around slowly, leaning against the cubicle entry with the world-weary air of all young up-and-coming executives forced to endure underlings more than twenty years their senior who don't understand that getting laid on Friday night is an imperative. I picked up the sheet and waved it. "What is this?"

He sighed, eager to be away and in search of the elusive *amore* eel. "One of the networks is starting a retrospective on some old spook series from the 50s." He said it like it predated the ice age.

"You mean before the peacock brought everything to us in living color and the market for black-and-white shows dropped stone dead?"

He rolled his eyes, having heard my diatribe before, and unable to comprehend how anyone might prefer black-and-white to color. "With the boom in sci-fi and horror, they want to exhume the entire run for broadcast. Just between you, me and the woodwork, I think it's a dumb idea. The only people awake that late who might be interested in watching some old black and white crapola are hookers, junkies, depressed housewives and –" His fingers snapped. "Old farts who can't get lucky." He gifted me with a final pitying look and walked away.

I held my breath until his footsteps faded, flipped him a double-handed bird, and then read the chit. *Night Walk* #570908. 'The Litonai Chant.'

ᘓ

I had no difficulty locating the episode. I remembered *Night Walk* as a program that scared the crap out of my then seven-year-old self. Every week, I begged Mom to let me stay up late, promising not to come crying if it gave me nightmares and invariably breaking that promise. Producer and host G.R. Easton had died in the middle of the first season. The series tried to limp through a second season without him, but the episodes lacked Easton's flair and vitality, and the show was cancelled shortly thereafter. I suffered a brief mourning period before moving on to other interests, but I never forgot *Night Walk*. Those were magic memories for me, and Easton remained a personal hero.

While the film cleaned, I set up the vault projector to give it a run-through. There was little sense in pissing off the network by sending over something that had deteriorated past the point of viewing. If 'The Litonai Chant' was trash, I'd pull another episode and send it instead, with a short note explaining the substitution. Besides, how could I pass up the opportunity to watch it again after all these years?

So, sprockets all on the pegs, clamps down, gate secure, arc lamp lit, motor started, damper open and... *presto!*

A black screen, a faint suggestion of background music, and the cool measured voice-over of G.R. Easton, just as I remembered. *"If you walk at night, you see things. Things of beauty. Things of mystery. Things of terror."* Fade to a moonlit country road. *"The things you take comfort in by day cease to exist... and you are left alone. Unprotected. Come with me... if you dare."*

Cut to a well-lit study, tastefully appointed with leather furniture and heavy mahogany tables, the walls lined with books and decorated with familiar works of art. A rich room, a room well-earned. An elderly gentleman sits in a chair drawn close to the blazing hearth, head bent in study over the time-worn cover of an ancient text. *"Mr. Alfred Lynde has received the anonymous gift of a curious old book. He doesn't yet know what's inside, but in a moment he... and you... will open those musty, moldering pages... and take the Night Walk."*

Oh, this was wonderful! Imagine a television show directed by Val Lewton (the original *Cat People*, remember?) with effects by Willis O'Brien (the fellow who taught Ray Harryhausen), and Conrad Hall working camera six years before he went over to *The Outer Limits*. I never saw the end credits, so I don't know if any of them worked on this show, but I could believe it. This was television at its finest!

The screen cut to black, the titles faded up, and we were back with the show. Lynde and his wife Abigail work to translate the book. It's written in some esoteric language they recognize in bits and pieces, but can't quite crack. The show had little physical action (certainly not enough to hold the attention span of today's television viewing troglodytes), but the camera angles, music and lighting blended to create a mood of such impending doom that I felt the hair rise on my neck.

Abigail labors methodically, maintaining a cool and scholarly air. Her husband is mercurial, quick-tempered, frustrated by limitations. After much effort, they translate a few words and the text begins to flow together. The book reveals itself to be a set of arcane rituals to bring back the dead from a purgatory called Talionis, so named for *lex talionis*, the Roman law of retaliation.

If you're any kind of horror buff at all, you know what happens next. "For the good of all and in the interest of science," Lynde must attempt one of these chants. Abigail is the antithesis of the typical 1950s female character. Instead of screaming, "No, darling! There are things mankind was not meant to know!" she smiles with brave confidence and urges her husband on his quest.

I could almost *smell* the tragedy ahead! It was in every somber, orchestrated note and moody, weird-angled shot. My arms pimpled with gooseflesh as Lynde began the chant. A long shot from below the book shows his face bathed in flickering firelight as he intones the words, hands moving in the prescribed patterns. Damn, but they are ugly words, guttural and full of power.

When he finishes, there's a pause, the sound-track thrumming with the high-pitched, almost inaudible cry of violins. Husband and wife look around, but nothing has appeared. Disappointment and disgust at his own naiveté rake furrows in Lynde's face like invisible claws...

...and then *something* materializes in the shadows behind them. There is a quick close-up, hardly more than a brief flash-shot to register its appearance and still stay within the 1950s Television Code boundaries of good taste, but *son-of-a-bitch!* Whoever did the special effects on this monstrosity deserved more accolades than I could give. It looked like three mythological creatures force-fed through a wood-chipper and reassembled by a demented five-year-old. Words cheapen the reality of it, but the bastard scared me so much that I stopped the film and flipped on the lights.

I know such behavior seems ridiculous coming from a man firmly into his fifth decade, but you try watching *any* other show from the 1950s, something like *Basil DuBois' Boat of Terror*, and you'll see people talking for fifteen minutes about "a monstrously obscene and hideous horror!" before they show you a ten-dollar-a-day extra lurching around in a papier-mâché costume. What I'd just seen wasn't like that. This was something to make any number of present-day creature shops gnaw their nail beds in envy.

I sat for several minutes feeling stupid as I worked up the nerve to finish watching the film. Just as I finally reached for the switch, footsteps sounded in the vault behind me. I suffered a second's spooking and then an embarrassing rush of relief. It must be one of the security guards. Maybe he'd take a break from rounds and watch the rest of the show with me... out of curiosity, of course.

Then there came a voice – and it was *that* voice, *his* voice, familiar because I'd just heard it. "Good evening, sir."

Years from now, they'll still be able to see my toe prints in the concrete floor. My breath didn't just die in my lungs, it turned to lead. Unable to speak, let alone yell, I turned around fast, hoping this was some sort of joke at my expense.

Honest to God.

Had to be.

Couldn't be, but was.

This was not the Easton of my memories – the dapper, well-dressed, middle-aged wizard of film. This was an Easton old beyond his years, the grey skin of his face eroded not by physical decay but by something deeper than his soul. Nattily attired in a 50's era suit, he folded his arms and leaned against one of the racks. It shifted a little, taking his weight, and I went cold. This was no ghost, no *chimera*, no bit of underdone potato.

"G.R. Easton," he said by way of introduction, his head tipping in a slight nod. Before I could even attempt to respond, he shouldered away from the rack and stepped closer to run a finger along the top of the projector, leaving a faint track in the thin layer of dust. "Maxwell Lewis was a damned fine script writer, don't you think? Maybe one of the best in the business, though I never told him so. Instead, I tweaked whatever he sent to me. Not because the work needed it, you understand; only to put my mark on it. To remind him who was boss." A smile of self-loathing touched the corners of his mouth. "Like some top dog pissing in the weeds. He tolerated it admirably well until I extended my attentions beyond the written word to a certain young woman with whom he was involved." Easton's smile grew ironic. "It was always about a woman back in those days," he murmured, and then sighed.

His finger circumnavigated the reel of the projector. "When Max first wrote the script he didn't pen in the chant, you know, just left notes that one would be added later, he'd come up with something. Shortly after, we had our big blow-up over the girl and he quit the project. We hadn't yet reached that point in filming, so when the time came I tried to write the chant myself, but everything sounded comical, ridiculous. I considered hiring another writer and then got this brainstorm to call Max, beg his help, say I couldn't do it without him, didn't he want his baby to be *all* his baby? I promised him I wouldn't touch a word this time, that we'd film whatever he wrote just the way he gave it to us."

Easton picked up the empty film canister, tilting it to read the cover label, and his smile grew sad. "Max was amenable to the idea, though he was in the middle of another project. He asked for twenty-four hours to 'get it right.'" Easton dropped the canister and I cringed as it clanged against the cement floor. "I agreed like some king granting a boon to a peasant. What an ass I was."

He turned to face the empty screen. "To stay on schedule, we went ahead with filming. Everything but the chant scene was shot by the time Max delivered the words." A faraway look came into Easton's eyes. "We started filming and suddenly I felt a grinding... here." The fingers of one hand splayed across his chest. "The pain hit and I turned, dropping to my knees. Max stood there, watching it happen, and I saw in his eyes that he *knew* what was happening. He'd done it on purpose." He shrugged. "And that was it for me. Dead before I hit the floor." He glanced about, absently noting the racks of movies disappearing into the gloom. "Turned out the little bastard was smarter than I gave him credit for."

I finally found my voice. "What do you mean?"

"There are two chants in the final film, did you know that?"

I shook my head, but I don't think he noticed.

"The first, as you've witnessed, brings me back from the dead. The second, at the end of the film when our hero saves as much of the day as remains, returns me from whence I came." He paused, then added, "It hurts," with a matter-of-factness that chilled me to the bone.

"I've been told by those in the know," he continued, tipping me an acerbic wink, his mouth pinched with bitterness. "That the pain magnifies in direct proportion to the number of voices repeating the chant. Apparently every television represents a single voice. It resonates with the viewer's psychic energy or something." He waved a hand. "I don't pretend to understand it."

A sudden shudder wrenched through him and the sardonic, self-deprecating manufactured grace was subsumed by an old man's exhaustion and fear. Despair closed his eyes and devoured the flesh of his cheeks. There was moisture at the corner of one folded eyelid as he whispered, "Haven't I paid enough?"

Despite his errors, despite his character flaws and the shitty way he'd treated Max Lewis, I felt nothing but compassion for this ruined man. The networks were notorious for using old shows as late-night filler, so how often had this happened to him? How many times had he been wrenched from one world to the other and back again?

Sudden horror blossomed in me like a black rose. I must have made a noise, because Easton's eyes sprang open. "What? What is it?"

I shook my head, not because I didn't want to tell him (though I didn't, God help me I didn't), but because the horror was too immense. "The network has recalled *Night Walk*. They want to run the series, run 'Latonai Chant,' for better than eighty-five million households…"

If I'd thought he couldn't look worse than he did, I was wrong. Wrinkles on his face turned to caverns, grey skin turned to eggshell. He staggered back against the wall and his legs gave out, tumbling him to the floor in a boneless heap, a marionette with cut strings. An unearthly wail, thin and thready, passed his lips like a damned soul seeking escape.

We stayed that way for I don't know how long — Easton sprawled on the floor, me still in my chair, uncertain what to do, both of us silent. Finally, I said, "I can hide it. Put it away someplace where it won't be found. Hell, just stick it back in the rack and tell them it doesn't exist anymore, send over another episode in its place."

"Faint reprieve until someone else is sent to hunt up an episode or roots around on a dusty shelf."

I inhaled slowly and asked a hateful question, terrified of the answer but knowing that, once offered, the deed would have to be done. "Do you want me to destroy it?"

Easton heaved a breath that was more sob than sigh. "I've asked myself more than once why I haven't burned the damned thing. There have certainly been opportunities. But it was the last piece of work I did, maybe the best, and I..." He shrugged. "I don't suppose you'd understand."

I smiled. There was no real warmth in it, but I shared it with a kindred soul. "I've spent more than twenty years of my life protecting the past. So much has already been lost." The last show of *UFO*. Three *Twilight Zone* episodes that no one has seen in more than 17 years. The episodes that solved the mystery in *A Crooked Mile*. "I understand better than you know."

We lapsed again into silence and more time passed before I rose, took the reel off the machine, put it back into its canister, and snugged down the lid. I glanced at my watch. Eight o'clock. Was that all? I felt like I'd been in the vault for days. "It's Friday night. The building is closed until Monday morning, when this reel is due at the network. Until then, there shouldn't be much traffic in here other than the occasional security guard you'll have to avoid. I'll be back as soon as I can." I looked down at the canister in my hands and then impulsively thrust it at him. "You hang on to this."

He took it like it might, without warning, sprout teeth and savage him. "What's on your mind, Mister..." A thin parody of the old Easton surfaced. "I'm afraid that we've never been properly introduced."

"Andrew Underhill." I didn't shake his offered hand, afraid of how it might feel. After a moment, he withdrew it, seeming to understand and taking no offense. "I'm going to try to help you. Without destroying your film."

He shook his head with a weariness that went beyond bone and flesh. "What can you possibly do to help me, Mr. Underhill, that I haven't thought of and tried myself?"

"Find Max Lewis."

଼

My worst fears – that Maxwell Lewis was dead, unlisted, or moved from the L.A. area – proved unfounded. The operator – a patient, saintly woman who was more than willing to help me locate a dearly beloved uncle with whom I'd lost touch – gave me several listings under Lewis. His was the third number I tried.

The phone picked up on the fourth ring. "Hello?" The voice was hale and hearty. What would he be now, in his mid-seventies maybe? Certainly not old by today's standards.

"Is this Mr. Maxwell Lewis?"

There was a resigned sigh. "What treasure have I won today, young man?"

I chuckled, liking his style. "Nothing from me, I'm afraid. Sir, my name is Andrew Underhill. I work at the Library of Congress in Washington."

"Well, you're calling from a long way, Mr. Underhill. What can I do for you?"

"Sir, I work in the Department of Copyright, in the Motion Picture Division. I'd like to talk to you about your work."

"Really?" He sounded pleased. "I didn't imagine that they kept track of old, mothballed script writers."

"Actually, Mr. Lewis, I'm calling about something you wrote in the late 50s for a Syndicom series." My heart began to pound.

"I did a lot of work for them." His voice sounded nostalgic. "They were just about the top payers at the time. Nice bunch of folks for the most part."

"Yes, sir. What I'm interested in is one of the shows you did for *Night Watch*. It's called 'The Litonai Chant.'"

I heard Lewis's breathing on the other end – shallow, rapid. "I don't have any memory of a piece by that name, Mr. Underhill." His voice was no longer friendly. "You must have the wrong man."

"Mr. Lewis!" If he hung up now, I'd never get him back. "I watched that episode this afternoon. And I met G. R. Easton."

The phone line did not go dead, but the silence stretched on for so long that I was afraid I'd killed him with the shock. He drew a shuddery breath. "You're crazy. Easton's dead. He's been dead for forty years."

"I think you know that's not entirely true, sir." My palms were sweating.

His voice crackled. "Easton had a heart attack and died the day he finished filming 'The Litonai Chant!' That doesn't mean I had anyth –"

I talked fast, words tumbling, hoping to get it all out before he slammed down the receiver. "You supplied the words to the chant at the last minute, when Easton couldn't come up with any on his own. You were angry because he'd seduced a woman you were dating, someone you were maybe serious about, and he ruined it. He treated you like shit, but when you had the chance to work on the script one more time you took it because that was the only way to get back at him as badly as you wanted to. So you sent him to Talionis."

41

Softly, "Dear God." Now he sounded old.

"You've had revenge for forty years, Mister Lewis, every time that episode airs as late-night fodder for insomniacs. Did you know that the pain grows, resonating and echoing with each voice added?" Silence. "Did you know that each television is a voice? What G.R. Easton did to you was wrong and I can't blame you for feeling as you did. But, Mr. Lewis, the network plans to air that program on Monday night to over eighty-five million homes."

I imagined him, three thousand miles away, sitting in his favorite chair in a sunny corner of the living room, eyes closed, the phone pressed to his ear. He'd have white hair, fine as milkweed silk above each ear, and wrinkles around his eyes and mouth. After today, those lines would be deeper.

Finally, he spoke. "What do you expect me to do, Mister Underhill?"

ೞ

I was back at the Library just after midnight. The guards, used to my odd hours, waved me through after making me promise to join them for a late night pizza that I had no intention of eating. Down in the vault, I eased open the door and called softly. "Mr. Easton?"

He came out of the stacks, shadow on shadow, and studied my face, the reel of film still in his arms. "What have you been up to, young man?"

I smiled. "It's been a lot of years since anyone called me that." Shedding my jacket, I took the reel from him and began to set up 'The Litonai Chant' to run one last time. "I talked to Maxwell

Lewis. He told me how to finish this and free you for good."

"So the son of a bitch is still alive, is he?" Easton's expression clouded. "Do you honestly think you can trust him? How do you know that this won't make things worse than they already are?"

I thought back on the conversation, the sound of Lewis's voice, the explicit directions, the tears and self-recrimination that came at the end. "We can trust him."

Easton looked dubious. "All right, Mr. Underhill. I hope you're right."

"I believe I am, sir." Projector ready, I wiped my palm on my slacks and held out my right hand. "It's been a pleasure to meet you, Mr. Easton."

He looked at my hand with surprise, then up into my eyes. A genuine smile graced his old face as his hand met mine. "Greg, please. And the pleasure has been mine, Andrew."

"It's Andy to my friends."

He nodded. "Andy, then. Thank you. What do you want me to do?"

"Turn off the lights and stand to one side. I'll take care of everything else." He stepped to the wall and the room went dark but for the red glow of the EXIT signs. Breathing a silent prayer, hoping that my gut was right in telling me that I could trust Max Lewis, I turned on the projector and watched Easton watch the remainder of his swan song, his face bathed in the lambent light of the projector. I will never forget his expression – love, longing, pride – and regret more profound than I could have imagined.

As Alfred Lynde began to recite the awful, hellish words of the second chant – the chant that would save the world – I joined in, flicking off the sound and continuing, not in the scripted words as filmed, but with new ones, words given to me by Maxwell Lewis. Agony ground in my chest like broken glass. Gasping, I kept chanting, making the hand motions as Lewis had described them. Panicked, Easton reached for me, but he was already fading and his hands slid *through* me, an instant's soft, cooling balm on the inferno of my heart. At the last moment, before he was gone entirely, I wrenched the film from the projector and flung it at him. He caught it, staggering back, holding it to his chest like a life preserver. Before he disappeared, bright light bloomed behind him, illuminating the exquisite relief on his face.

And for him, at least, there was no pain.

Moonwalk

The first time it happens – coming back late, disheveled and smelling bad – they let it pass and hope that it's a one-time aberration, something he'll outgrow. He's young, after all, and not yet entirely accountable for his behavior. Besides, he's always been strange, given to moody spells and daydreaming, roaming while others sleep, lethargic when the rest are about their business. A solitary figure, he lingers at the back of things, ever the observer, never the aggressor. Some in the family believe he is solitary too often and needs work to make him fit in, but with what work can he be trusted? His dull regard, pupils fixed, makes them nervous, makes them wonder if he's damaged in his head somehow. And if a touch of the frantic comes into that gaze from time to time, they turn their heads and let it pass along with his other odd ways, telling themselves that things will be better once he's grown.

The second time – reeking of poisons and unnamable acts – they punish him. Snubbed by even the youngest, he is temporarily excluded from the family. Outside looking in, he whines like a baby and pees himself until the nose-wrinkling stench of his own urine overrides the other odors. When he is forgiven and allowed to return, he expresses his gratitude by fawning like a beaten dog, going from one to the other, even to the children, apologizing, begging forgiveness. It's an ugly display that makes the adults turn aside in disgust.

The third time, he is gone a week (they hope for good, though no one says it), and crawls home streaked with blood, smelling of sex and

45

foreign things. Beneath the unforgiving horns of the waning moon they gather, immune now to the roll of his beseeching eyes. Shiny pink skin catches the light where hair is missing, not yet grown back. Fingers like fat, naked worms peek from between ragged tufts of fur, shortening as they watch, turning into proper toes. Flat, useless teeth – flecked with who knows what grossness – grow long and pull back his darkening lips into a servile grin. Tail tucked tight against his human ass, he makes the mistake of whining.

Blood sprays across the snow in a crimson fan, breaking the moon's light into sparkling shards. He screams as they circle, driving him away. When his pleading grows tedious, they close in and savage him.

Later, passing away beneath the moon's darkening shadow, the wolf pack leaves behind the changeling corpse of the one who was always too different.

Brother's Keeper

"I don't know what to do."

Arms folded tight across her chest, Sarah O'Connor stared through the window at the yard. Wind blew sand into small twisters that danced spirals around the sun-bleached, warped boards of the wagon, the empty shafts canted to rest on the hard-packed earth. Rain was on the way; thunderheads massed in the distance, grey on black on purple, gravid with welcome moisture. Sometime today, with any luck, they'd loose their hoarded wealth onto the farm.

Her gaze slid from the swollen clouds to the back of the young woman who sat in the yard, staring into the distance, long dark hair whipping in the rising wind. Sarah couldn't see Elizabeth Brown's face, but didn't need to in order to see the tear tracks gone gritty with blown dirt.

"Sarah?"

God but how she'd come to hate the sound of her brother's voice. "What?"

"I don't know what to do," he repeated, as if she hadn't heard him before.

She turned to look at him – tall, lean, ginger-haired. Handsome, she supposed. Muscled, but not as much as he would have been had he actually put himself to use. "I think that's obvious."

He winced at her tone, a cur whipped back for misbehavior, chewing a shoe or soiling a rug. Lawrence had shit where he lived, getting a baby on a hired girl a hair's breadth out of childhood.

Blue eyes watched her, hopeful and wary by turns. Did he expect her to rescue him? Well, yes,

47

she supposed he did. She'd rescued him since they were children – made excuses for him, took on bullies in the school yard, stood up to Father's rages when his son's spoiled nature drove the older man to the brink of violence. They'd stopped being children a long time ago, but nothing had changed. She doubted that it ever would, and whose fault was that?

But this was different.

"I don't want to marry Elizabeth."

"Stop whining." Sarah glanced out the window at the girl, who hadn't moved. Her back was rigid, hands placed on knees parted (as she'd parted them for Lawrence?) to allow room for her growing belly. Head lifted, Elizabeth let the wind scour her cheeks raw. Penance? Her hair would be a rat's nest of knots and snarls when she finally came indoors. It would take Sarah hours to comb it free. She turned back to her brother. "You should have thought of that. You're not so stupid that you don't know where babies come from."

Lawrence cringed again and it made her want to slap him. "She--"

A hand came up, not to strike (doing that would be like punching a dumb beast), but to point a rigid finger. "Don't you dare! Elizabeth's little more than a child. She can hardly be held accountable for her own actions. Don't compound the offense by making her take on the responsibility of yours as well." She breathed tight through her nose, quelling her anger. "You have to decide what you *are* going to do."

He dropped his gaze, boots scuffing Mother's braided rug like a child caught with his finger in the Sunday pie. "I don't want to marry Elizabeth."

"So you said." When he remained silent, Sarah walked to another window and rested her arms on the rails, chin on her arms. This view looked out onto the back yard, the empty clothesline, discarded oddments of farm equipment, a few chickens scratching the ground. All the way to the distant mountains – mottled in colors like the storm clouds – the land was theirs.

No, not *theirs*. If work and sweat and blood made the land your own, it was hers by right. But by law? That was another matter altogether. Father's desire to create a worthy heir out of his son had compelled him to leave the place to Lawrence. He put Sarah into her younger brother's keeping until the day she might marry, although he made clear his doubts in that regard. Sarah worked the land, bred the beeves, made repairs, shot predators, bartered for supplies, hired hands when she could afford to, and took in orphaned Elizabeth to wash and clean, cook and gather eggs. Lawrence went to town, hung around with his friends, drank too much, bedded whores with money stolen from the kitchen crock, and got a child pregnant. "Do you expect her to raise the baby alone?" Sarah spoke to the window. Her breath fogged the glass, softening her reflection.

"We could send her away."

"Turn her out, you mean."

"No." Lawrence amended hurriedly. "We can give her some money, send her off to a city where no one knows her."

Or you. Make the problem disappear, sister. Vanish the discomfort, Sarah. Abracadabra the difficulty. She was so tired of this, so tired of Lawrence. "A city," she echoed dully. "Where they'll starve, or the authorities will take away the baby, or

49

Elizabeth will be passed around among men (*like you*) until there's nothing left to die in the gutter except the diseased husk of a girl old before her time."

It had grown dark, the storm coming on faster than she'd guessed. The chickens were straggling toward the barn, looking to roost. The horses had their rumps toward the wind, heads bowed, cropping a few last mouthfuls of sparse fodder before seeking shelter under the lean-to.

Lawrence was reflected in the glass, eyes pleading, but she recognized the glint of rapaciousness in their depths. This was the only determination he possessed — that nothing bothersome ever touch him.

We could send her away.

...send her away...

Sarah sighed and straightened, let her arms fall to her sides, and turned to face him. "I suppose it's the only solution."

"It is?" His chin came up a fraction, a little boy avoiding punishment once more.

"What choice do we have? It's your farm, after all. It's not as if--"

Lawrence's features contorted and he slapped the palm of his hand down on the table. "I *hate* this farm." It was true; he did. Always had. Hated everything about it, except the money it made. He worked toward its good only when forced to, and those occasions were rare since the fruits of his labor were often so poor that the argument wasn't worth the bother. His brows drew together, confused. "'Not as if' what?"

She shook her head slightly and slid her hands into her apron pockets. "Nothing. Better to forget about it."

"Not as if what, Sarah?" he persisted.

"Well, it's not as if *you* would leave."

"Me?"

"I didn't mean it that way. It's not like you're trapped here. Of course you could leave if you wanted to. You're a grown man and can do as you please."

"But Father left the farm to *me*."

"Yes, he did. That's right. But he never said that you had to stay here in order to own it. He never said you had to *live* here."

Lawrence's face lit with growing delight at the notion and all that it implied. "I can go live in the city?" His gaze focused inward, seeing imagined sights. His tongue flicked over his lips, savoring imagined delights. "Which city should I go to, Sarah?"

"Any city you like, I expect. Chicago. Boston. New York. Santa Fe." A rumble of thunder made them both jump. Sarah looked out as a fork of distant lightning lit the landscape. Elizabeth did not stir, not even when raindrops began to pock the dusty ground, leaving tiny craters of moisture.

"What about the farm? Do you think I could sell it for a lot of money?"

Sarah gave it some thought. "Probably not much. There's no market for it right now. Anyway, what you'd make off a sale wouldn't last very long in the city. Things there are expensive." She watched his brows draw together. He was unhappy, petulant, a little boy ready to have a tantrum. "But..."

"What?" His look immediately lightened and grew eager, trusting her to steer him right.

"Well, if you leave, I'll still need a place to live. I'm too old to try living in the city. Besides, having a big sister along would ruin all your fun."

Lawrence was more than willing to agree with that. "Father said I was supposed to take care of you." His tone was righteous.

Sarah remembered a time when, angered by some slight, Lawrence had driven her off the place. Three days alone with no one to cook and clean and take care of the farm had sent him after her, apologizing, begging her to return. "Yes, he did, so why not let me stay here? I can run the place and send you money every month."

He mulled that over, jaw working like he tasted something sweet. "What about Elizabeth? My leaving doesn't take care of her problem."

Her problem. Like she'd gotten pregnant all on her lonesome. "Well, I can't run the farm by myself. You'll be gone, and she *has* been good help. No one in town knows she's pregnant. I can keep her here until the birth and we'll make up some story to explain the baby." As if anyone in town couldn't figure it out for themselves.

Lawrence's eyes lit. "Like maybe someone passing through left it on the doorstep!"

"That's a wonderful idea! We'll do it just like that."

He chewed his lip, fidgeting. "Should I leave today?"

"Why not? The city is calling you."

"But it's *raining*." The water had become a steady drumming on the roof. Sarah found it soothing, enough to make her want to curl up like a cat and nap away the afternoon. Maybe she would, if she could ever get him gone.

"Wear Father's old waxed duster. That'll keep you dry for the ride into town. You can leave the horse at the blacksmith's and then take your pick of either the mail coach or the train. I'll reclaim the horse the next time I go in for supplies."

Lawrence's eyes narrowed a fraction. "What about money? You said cities are expensive."

Sarah waved an airy hand. "Take what's in the kitchen crock. Just leave me enough to buy flour and salt."

Once Lawrence had a goal in mind, he set right to it. While Sarah packed a rucksack with clothing and food, she watched out of the corner of her eye as he scooped every last cent out of the kitchen jar and put it back empty. That was all right. She'd been skimming the household finances for years. Outside, Elizabeth was a ghost in the grey fall of rain, her hair plastered to her back, dress clinging to the rounded curves of her body.

"Sarah?"

"Yes?"

"I want the Henry."

Startled, her gaze jumped to the fireplace where the rifle hung on two brackets over the mantle, brass points gleaming. She had saved egg money in order to buy it, and used it to bring wild meat to their table, frighten off the occasional low-life drifter, and dispatch vermin. Her heart tripped in her chest. "Whatever for?" she asked, keeping her voice light. "You don't need a gun like that in the city."

"What if someone tries to hold me up on the way into town? What if I see a bear?"

"Neither of those things is likely to happen."

"What if someone tries to rob the stage or the train?"

"Trains and stages have guards. And you have your Colt."

"You keep the Colt. I *want* the Henry."

Sarah knew that tone. There was no use pushing the issue. She nodded. "All right. But do me a favor?"

"What?" Guardedly.

"Say goodbye to Elizabeth. Let her know you're leaving. Tell her that she has a place to stay. You can even say that you're going away as a favor to her."

He liked that idea. "All right." He shrugged into the waterproof and tugged down his wide-brimmed hat. "Goodbye, Sarah." He hugged her.

"I'll tack up your horse and meet you out back with your things," she said into his chest. She watched from the window as he crossed the yard and halted beside Elizabeth, and stopped watching as he bent to speak into the girl's ear. Pulling on a jacket, she took the Henry down and dashed out the back door. It took only a moment to throw a blanket and saddle onto Lawrence's roan, ease the bit into its mouth, tie on the rucksack, and slide the rifle into its scabbard.

Her fingers traced patterns on the horse's wet hide. Even with the money she'd send, she knew Lawrence would sell the gelding in a month or two, likely for far less than the animal was worth. The Henry, beautiful thing that it was, would follow suit. And then? Why, then Lawrence would want more money, of course. And when she didn't send it, or couldn't, he'd come home.

Withdrawing the Henry from the scabbard, she checked the ammunition as the sound of boots splashing up water came around the house to meet her.

Elizabeth, who never moved while telling Sarah she was pregnant, who did not stir when Lawrence told her he didn't love her or want to marry her, who stayed motionless as rock when he bid her goodbye, flew around the corner of the house as the echo of the gunshot was swallowed by the storm. Stumbling to a halt, she starred, wild-eyed, at Lawrence – face-down in the mud, feet splayed, tendrils of blood mixing with the rain – and raised her eyes.

Sarah returned the girl's gaze with no show of emotion. Lowering the rifle from her shoulder, she cradled it in the crook of one arm and studied her brother's body. "Guess I'd better find a shovel," she said, and walked off toward the barn.

Centaur

There must have been thirty of them. Horses, caught in a moment of exuberance, manes streaming from arched necks, whipped by the wind of their passage, flagged tails held high. Hooves beat the earth in a thundering, primal pulse as they circled the pasture. Bursting through morning mist as high as their shoulders, they looked like something ancient materializing out of the past, Indian ponies on stampede.

You see? That's the sort of talk that gets you into trouble.

Joel's foot lifted from the gas, slowing the pickup, letting it coast onto the narrow shoulder of the back-country road, and stop. Engine idling, one booted foot gently working to keep the old girl from stalling out, he watched the animals.

God, but they were beautiful. Round haunches bunched and flexed as hooves kicked up clods of earth and tossed them high. Broad chests worked, slick with sweat, and nostrils flared, drawing in huge gulps of air. They charged from one end of the field, running flat out until nearly colliding with the opposite fence, and then turned as one *(the horses, flock-like, wheel as birds...Stop it!)* and raced back. Over and over, they repeated the cycle – charge, wheel, race – clearly reveling in the cloudless day, the feel of wind against their faces...

Freedom. Joel felt a pang in his chest.

One horse in particular caught his eye – brown and white, flashy-looking, with a stripy mane and tail. A *pinto* he remembered them being called. Or was this a *paint*? He couldn't remember the

56

difference. This animal was swifter than the rest, the most agile and sure-footed, taking the lead by a full length, long legs pistoning, neck outstretched to match his stride and then arching in a fit of cockiness as he kicked his heels and whinnied. He led the herd like something out of mythology, born of the goddess Epona and a race whose name was long-forgotten. Head high, his eyes were trained not on the approaching fence, but on the range beyond and the horizon.

He sees the future, Joel thought. *And likes what he sees.*

Another pang, this one of envy. Only that morning, he and Bonnie had argued again. Lately, it seemed there was always something to argue about – money, whether or not to have a baby, the new washer and dryer she wanted. In Bonnie's eyes, Joel could do nothing right.

He was a good man. Rock solid, dependable, honest. He held down two jobs to make ends meet, jobs he hated. Construction paid well, when there was work to be had, but it was hot, heavy, ball-busting employment and the foreman was forever ragging on Joel, finding fault. The second job – custodial work at the high school – was a little better. It paid squat, but it was regular work and quiet after hours, leaving him time to write poetry and think, even though thinking wasn't always a good idea. He didn't chase women, he didn't do drugs, and his once-a-week beer with Ross and the guys never went beyond two. He spent days off and down-time busting his fanny to keep the house from collapsing around their ears, bartering for lumber, plumbing supplies, whatever they needed. Bonnie hung on to her part-time cashier job at the drugstore and never considered looking for something with more hours and some benefits. She sat at home, drinking diet soda, watching infomercials and the *"Love is Everywhere"* channel, leafing through catalogs and picking out items they could never afford. And complaining. Bonnie might be lazy in a lot of areas, but she had a Grade A mouth on her that never took a vacation.

03

It hadn't always been that way. In the beginning, things between them were great, better than great. They'd met at the local drive-in. He was there with Tracy Scott, rumored to be the most miserly girl in town. She hung onto her virginity and her cash with a rock-hard fist and used it (the cash; he didn't know about the virginity) to finally hop a bus out of town. Last Joel heard she was a nurse working with cancer patients, making good money, and married to a doctor.

Nineteen-year-old Bonnie was there with Red Adams, an older, lanky, hard-muscled pseudo-cowboy who wore tight jeans, boots, and a big belt buckle but (as far as Joel knew) had never sat a horse. They were with a gang, drinking beer out of the back of Red's old Mustang convertible. Joel watched them as he stood in line at the concession stand, waiting to buy Tracy some popcorn and a large soda for them to share. The group was boisterous, Red the noisiest of the lot, yee-hawing, shooting off his mouth, grabbing tit. Even from a distance, Joel could see Bonnie's embarrassment every time Red did it, cupping her breast and giving it a squeeze like it was something he owned. She'd slap his hands away in a pretend I'm-not-really-bothered manner, but her laughter was thin and Joel wondered why she tolerated Red's bullshit.

58

Arriving at the front of the line, Joel placed his order to the bored woman behind the counter. Her frowzy blonde hair was pulled up into a top-knot and her name tag, balanced precariously atop an enormous breast, read 'Darleen.' At the last minute he ordered "Nachos, too, please, with extra cheese." Maybe a little treat would warm Tracy to his affections. Darleen shot him a look, nodded so he'd know she'd heard, and kept working.

"Just *do* it!" That was Red, real loud now. Joel glanced over in time to see him swipe at Bonnie's face. She ducked so he missed her cheek, but he clocked her good and hard on the ear and she cried out. "Aw, quitcherbitchin'!" Red pushed money into her hand and gave her a shove. "Go get me some cigs. And a book of matches."

There was no one in line behind Joel. Bonnie reached past him to pull several napkins out of the dented stainless steel dispenser on the counter. Sniffing, she wiped her eyes and blew her nose. Darleen placed his food on the counter, he paid her, said thanks (she looked momentarily startled by the courtesy), and picked up the popcorn, drink and chips. Turning, he looked straight into Bonnie's eyes.

Magnified by tears, they seemed enormous and very blue. Her hair, sun-streaked blonde, was pulled back into a pony-tail. Her face, beneath too much makeup, was actually very pretty, and would be prettier yet if she let her freckles and bit of sunburn show through.

"What are you looking at?" she snarled, still dabbing at her eyes. Her ear, where Red had struck her, was scarlet.

Before he could stop himself, Joel said, "'Oh, thou art fairer than the evening air clad in the beauty of a thousand stars.'"

She frowned, confused. "What?"

"Shakespeare," he said, feeling his face go flush and warm with embarrassment. "*The Tragical History of Doctor Faustus.*"

"That's poetry."

He shrugged. "Yeah, I guess."

A tiny smile tugged up one corner of her mouth. Now, he knew, she'd make fun of him. They always did. "You like poetry?"

He took a deep breath, resigned to ridicule. "Yeah."

"Wow."

The word – said low and breathy – startled him. Her expression was not one of derision, but wonder. Seeing it made him brave. "I write some, too."

"You *write* poetry?" Wonder bloomed into amazement, fascination. "I never met a guy who wrote poetry before."

"I – "

"*BAAAAAH-NEEEEEEEE! Bonnie! Quit shootin' the shit! Get your ass moving and buy those cigs!*" Raucous laughter, followed by "Dumb bitch," said loud enough for all to hear.

Bonnie's cheeks flamed and she ducked her head, sliding past Joel to place her order and push the money across the counter. He turned to leave, hesitated, and turned back as she picked up the packet of smokes and the matches. "You don't have to put up with that."

She shook her head. "You don't know." Before he could reply, she shouldered past him with a brusque, "Mind your own business," and

60

went back to her group. Joel watched her for a moment and then headed for the car.

Three weeks later, Red took up with some waitress out at the truck stop, and Joel asked Bonnie out on their first date.

cs

Lost in thought, Joel pulled at his bottom lip. In the beginning, Bonnie liked his appreciation of poetry, liked that he'd recite passages to her as they drove around the countryside or ate at some roadside stand. Liked that he whispered it in her ear as they made out in his truck and, later, made love in his bed. When he grew brave enough to share his own work with her, she listened attentively, eyes wide in amazement that such words could come out of someone she knew, someone she *loved*.

But the good feelings, the attentiveness and amazement, went south. Not all at once, but bit by bit, trickling away like a tiny hole in the bottom of a bag of sugar, until all the sweet was gone. Bonnie went from loving his poetry to despising it. She resented the time he spent on it, dreamy-eyed and lost in the words. Most of all, she hated that he didn't do anything with it, didn't try to sell it somewhere. If Joel's poetry couldn't buy her the things she craved in life, what good was it?

Hugs and kisses, whispers at midnight, the touch of tender hands...those, too, vanished, replaced by silence, sarcasm, and avoidance.

A sharp whinny yanked Joel out of his reverie. As the herd approached the far fence again, the big pinto flung up his head and bellowed a challenge at the sky. Legs thrusting, he flung himself forward, outpacing the other horses with a

61

burst of incredible speed, ivory hooves pounding the earth like the beat of warrior drums. Haunches bunched, this time he did not wheel at the barrier, but vaulted into space, soaring over the confining timber. Landing hard, he stumbled, drawing Joel half out of the truck, afraid that the horse had broken a leg.

The herd milled, colliding with each other, rocking against the fence, confused by their leader's desertion. Giving his body a shake, the pinto glanced back at the herd, tossed his head again, this time in dismissal, and set off for the distant hills.

No longer bound by plowshare, cart-shaft, or governing rein, larger than imagining, winged with wind and sun, cloud and rain... The words ran pell-mell through Joel's head. Sighing, his heart heavy with both desire and regret, he put the truck into gear and drove to work.

○ଃ

Pulling into the driveway that night, Joel ran a jaundiced eye over the house and yard, tallying in his head the list of chores piling up in anticipation of the weekend. The lawn was a jungle. A half-dozen slats on the picket fence needed replacement and painting. The house could do with a coat of fresh, too, but that wasn't happening any time soon. The porch roof had a hole in it you could chuck a pumpkin through. The clothes hanging limp on the forlorn line strung between house and barn had been there for days and were now so full of blown sand that they needed to be re-laundered. And that was only the tip of the iceberg that was his life.

Parking behind Bonnie's beat-to-death Buick, Joel turned off the truck and sat for a moment, head tipped back against the seat, listening to the tick of the truck's cooling engine. He was sweaty, dirty, and sun-burned. Every muscle begged for sleep. *And his soul was weary beyond belief.* He smiled a little at the inadvertent rhyme.

Evinrude, the orange tabby who lived in the barn, came running for his nightly scratch. Joel paused to oblige the tom, smiling at the gusty roar of the cat's purr, and then mounted the front stoop. The door was propped open, letting in flies, letting out the ceaseless drone of the television. Bonnie was on the sway-seated couch dressed in shorts and a tank-top with no bra, wads of cotton between her toes, painting her nails the lurid pink of a carnivorous tropical flower. Her hair was drawn back from her face and secured by two small plastic butterfly barrettes. Something about the scene – Bonnie, the polish, the barrettes – clogged Joel's throat with love and longing, sadness and desire.

"Hey, hon."

Bonnie grunted, her glazed eyes never leaving the television as Bob Barker called another contestant to "come on down!"

The house was a mess, dusty and cluttered with the detritus of life left to lie where it dropped. Old newspapers, empty plastic grocery sacks, discarded socks, and dishes crusty with residue littered the room, spilling into the kitchen. Bonnie's pink work smock and pants were wadded into a corner of the couch with a tangle of pantyhose. Joel tried to keep the place tidy, but he was one man against a tsunami. Mama always said you couldn't shovel shit uphill with a slotted spoon, and she'd been right.

The only area where disorder was kept at bay, an oasis in the maelstrom of Hurricane Bonnie, was the corner that held Joel's brokeback recliner and a standing unit of three shelves filled with precious books.

"What's for dinner?"

She shrugged, reached out without looking, and tossed a take-out menu in his direction.

He bit back his irritation. "We don't have the money for take-out, Bonnie. I told you that. I had to put something on each of the bills as a show of good faith. I used the rest for groceries and gas."

She snorted like he'd done something stupid and shrugged a bony shoulder. "You try and make something out of the crap you bought."

"There's nothing wrong with what I bought, Bonnie. I got potatoes and rice, spaghetti, canned goods–"

"Then you fix it!" She shrieked, half-rising, hands balled into fists. One foot slid against the couch cushion, leaving a smear of polish across the upholstery and her toes. "Oh, *shit!*" She grabbed a tissue and a bottle of polish remover. "Goddamnit, Joel!"

Putting down his jacket and lunchbox, he toed off his boots, placed them neatly beside the door, and tried again. "How was work today?" He kept his voice low, modulated, unthreatening.

Bonnie dabbed at her toes, removing polish, and refused to look at him. "I called in sick."

Joel felt something inside him go *snap!* "Were you sick?"

"What's that supposed to mean?"

"The year's barely half over and you've already used up your paid sick days. If you don't work, you don't get paid. We need that money, Bonnie."

"I'm aware of that, Mister Know-It-All. Obviously, if I called in sick then I was *sick!*"

"You seem fine."

She glared at him and slowly rose from the couch. "Are you calling me a liar?"

He looked away, afraid to speak because if one hoarded word slipped free, they all would, and the results would be awful. His gaze skimmed over, and then registered, a soda can sitting on the bar between living room and kitchen. There was a cigarette butt crushed out on the lid. He hadn't bought soda this week. And neither he nor Bonnie smoked. "Who was here, Bon?"

She heaved a put-upon sigh. "*Now* what are you talking about?"

One step over the mountain of crap brought him to the bar. He lifted the can with two fingers and shook it, hearing the rattle of more butts inside. So that was why the door was open. He looked at her over his shoulder, and waited.

She cocked one hip and tossed her head, insolent. "I wanted a soda. So sue me."

"I didn't buy any soda."

"I went out to get one."

"While you were sick?" He couldn't keep the sarcasm from his voice. "Did you buy a pack of cigarettes, too?"

Something flickered in the depths of her eyes, but Bonnie shrugged as if none of it mattered. "There a law against it?"

"I didn't know you took up smoking."

"You just would have nagged me about it. What business is it of yours, anyway? I buy my own."

"With the money you don't make by calling in sick?" Something was growing inside him, a thing he couldn't name. His chest felt tight. On impulse, he turned, dropped the can, and strode toward the bedroom, past the couch and Bonnie's wadded up clothing.

A man's fingers toyed with the smock's zipper and slid it down between Bonnie's breasts so he could reach inside and touch the warm flesh. Hands on her hips, he kneaded the pink polyester slacks, shoved them down over her ass, taking the pantyhose with it, hooked his fingers into the white cotton panties...

Bonnie sprinted around the couch and grabbed at his arm. "Hey, Joel! Hey, honey, c'mon, let's not fight. What do you say we pop a couple of those chicken pot pies in the oven and while they're heating up we can do the nasty right here on the –"

He shook her off hard enough to send her staggering into the wall, and kicked open the bedroom door.

He'd made the bed before leaving for work. The habit was Joel's piss-poor way of making himself feel just a little in control of his life, having another small piece of the house look cared for and normal. Now the bedspread was puddled on the floor, the sheets rumpled and twisted. One pillow was up on end. The other was across the room, leaning against the closet door. Even the lampshades were crooked, like in a bad comedy.

Bonnie thrust herself between him and the bed. Her fingers tangled in the front of his shirt. "I

66

went back to bed after you left. I told you I was sick."

"What are you all hyped up about, Bon, if that's the truth?" He was amazed at how normal his voice sounded. "Don't I understand? Aren't I the one who *always* understands?" He looked past her and spied something in the middle of the mattress. Pain contorted his features. "Christ, Bonnie." His voice was part disgust, part moan of pain. "Couldn't you at least change the sheets when you were done?"

Her head whipped back and forth, checking the bed, looking at him. A million emotions sped across her face as she tried each one on and discarded it for the next. She settled on teary rage. "What are you saying, Joel? Are you accusing me of *cheating* on you?" She raised a hand as if to slap him, but something in his expression stopped her. Eyes welling, chin trembling like a child's, she shoved him out of the room and he let her. "Well, if that's what you think, then screw you! Sleep on the couch!" She slammed the door in his face and locked it.

From the bedroom came the wail of crocodile tears and the thud and thump of things being thrown. Joel listened for a moment and then turned away, unable to think what to do next. He barely made it to his chair before his legs gave out, spilling him into the torn and shabby fake leather. His skin went waxy and cold, his heart raced, and his hands palsied like an old man's. For a moment or two, he thought he might throw up. The spell passed, leaving him drained and hopeless, and he fell asleep to the sound of Bonnie's tantrum.

When he woke, the house was dark but for the bluish glow of the television where a comely vampire bride stalked the mortal hero. From behind the bedroom's closed door, he heard David Letterman on the little portable that sat on the dresser.

He was at a loss for what to do. Leave? The house was his; well, half his, since he'd insisted on putting Bonnie's name on the title when they got married. Kick her out? He thought he could get away with that, given her infidelity, but the notion – not so much of her *gone* as of *where* she would go – pained his heart so that he could hardly breathe.

He swung the recliner from side to side. First the television came into view (the hero had killed the vampire girl and was now after Dracula) and then the shelf of books. Television and books. Television and…

He reached out and took a battered poetry collection into his lap. The spine was broken, pages creased, half the back cover missing. The book had seen better days, once upon a time, long before he purchased it for fifty cents at a library sale.

Letting it fall open at random, he held it to catch the light from the television and read something by Wallace Stevens:

"He had said that everything possessed
The power to transform itself, or else,
And what meant more, to be transformed."

Joel stared at the television, but did not see the action being played out there. The thoughts which streamed through his head weren't practical. One might say they bordered on ludicrous. But they made more sense than anything else had in a long time.

಄

"Joel? *Joel-ee*?"

Bonnie couldn't believe she was standing in the rain beside the old Buick, calling across a greening field. Couldn't believe she accepted as truth the nonsense Ross told her yesterday afternoon. Still... She glanced at the old pickup parked on the side of the road, right where Joel must have left it over a week ago, and shook her head. Better to believe Ross's craziness then to accept...what? Kidnapping? Murder? Alien abduction? "*Jo-leeeeeee...*"

The horses stood bunched together in peaceful camaraderie, grazing under the fall of light rain, blocky teeth cropping at new grass. The *pock!* as their teeth met reminded Bonnie of a tennis ball being bounced on pavement. Long tails swished idly. There were no flies today to bother them. Their hides were glossy with wet, darkening their natural hues. She half expected to see the color running down their legs, like chalk pictures ruined in a downpour.

When she came out of the bedroom the morning after their fight, Joel was already gone. She'd called in sick again and spent the day cleaning the house, throwing out trash, doing laundry. She even cooked a meal – spaghetti and salad and garlic bread.

Joel didn't come home that night. She assumed he was off pouting somewhere and would drag his ass in late. She fell asleep to the sound of an old kung-fu movie and didn't wake until the telephone rang. It wasn't Joel, but Ross, catting around to see when she was free again. She'd said something – she couldn't remember what – and hung up.

When Joel didn't come home for three days, she went to the police and reported him missing. She answered the cop's questions: No, he hadn't seemed depressed. Sure, they had money problems. Didn't everyone? She lied when they asked about arguments and relationship difficulties. That was nobody's business. As it was, the cops weren't the ones to find the truck, but Ross, coming home from a fishing trip and taking what he thought was a short-cut along a rarely used back-country road. He'd recognized the vehicle and, knowing Joel was missing, had stopped to check for signs of foul play. There weren't any, but what he did find sent him to Bonnie and not the police. And now she was here.

Movement at the center of the herd quickened her heart, but it was only the animals shifting like a heavy current, moved by the whim of grass or wind. She remembered back to when she and Joel first got together. They'd been driving somewhere – *a dance? Picnic? Swimming?* – and a flock of geese had flown over, dark silhouettes chevroned against the overcast sky. Joel had jerked the truck onto the shoulder and flung open his door to stand with one foot inside, the other on the running board, face lifted as he tracked their progress. When he finally got back inside and closed the door, the look he turned on her was one of elation. "Honest to God, Bonnie," he said, putting the truck into gear and easing it back onto the road. "Animals are the purest form of poetry there is." At the time she'd thought him brilliant. Now it was...

Bullshit. And this is bullshit, too, and so is that dumb-ass Ross. All I'm getting out here is wet. She'd just have to accept that Joel was gone. It was just as well. If he hadn't left, she'd have been forced to sooner or later. Imagine trying to make a life with a man like him! She wondered why she'd bothered. She didn't know why he'd abandoned the truck, but was glad of it. It was old and beat up, but she could get a couple hundred for it, and more than that for the house.

Chin tucked inside the collar of her coat, Bonnie turned to get back into the car. That was when she saw him.

"Joel?"

He peered at her over the backs of the herd, his chin resting on the withers of a chestnut mare. He breathed deeply through his nose, but rain and distance conspired against him and he couldn't catch the woman's scent. Arms crossed in the pale yellow raincoat, she looked either angry or cold. Both maybe. He should at least go and say hello, all things being equal.

He moved through the herd, nudging them aside with hands gentle on shoulders and rounded rumps. When he stepped into the clear, she drew a sharp breath and her hands flew to her face, covering the open "O" of her mouth. He hobbled toward her, his gait uneven. His legs had developed an ache that wouldn't quit. It kept him up nights.

"Joel, oh Joelee..." Her voice was a low moan and she reached over the fence as if to embrace him. "What happened? Who did this? Did someone beat you up?"

He halted beyond the reach of her hands. "Bonnie." He said it with some effort. He hadn't talked for weeks and his voice was raspy. "No."

It took her a second to understand that he'd answered her question. "Well, then..." She waved a hand, perplexed. "Where the hell are your clothes?"

"Clothes?" He looked down. He was naked, penis hanging flaccid amid a thatch of dark hair. A fine, pale down covered most of his body. "Don't know."

"You don't *know*?" She slapped her hands onto her hips. "Don't play games with me, Joel. You don't come home. You don't call. The police can't find you. I think you're fucking *dead*! The bill collectors are driving me crazy –" She flung up her hands. "And Ross sees you running in a field, playing with horses..." Her voice grew strident. "What *happened* to you?"

He blinked at her. Rain beaded on his lashes and coursed in rivulets down the length of his body. "'I tell thee what, Hal, if I tell thee a lie, spit in my face; call me horse.'"

"*What*?"

"Shakespeare. Henry the Fourth." He stamped his feet and drops of mud splashed up, spotting his flesh where faint marks like enormous pale bruises showed.

"What the hell are those?" She pointed. "Oh, my God, baby, did someone hurt you? Were you mugged?"

He shook his head. "No."

She waited, but he said nothing more. "Don't you dare stand there like some stupid retard, like a dumb beast, and tell me 'no' and expect me to just accept it. I want to know what's going on."

He reached back to scratch the base of his spine. "'If wishes were horses, beggars might ride.' Ray, *English Proverbs*."

She sputtered in confusion and rage. "Go to Hell! You owe me an explanation after all the shit I've put up with. You want a divorce, is that it? You think if you pretend to be crazy, I'll feel sorry for you and won't take you to the cleaners? Ha!" She threw up her head like a mare on alert. The movement spooked him and he jigged sideways. "It's not like you're worth anything, anyway. Never have been, never will be. I don't know why I –"

Her words continued, droning in the background like the undertone of bees on a hot summer day. As with the bees, he paid them no mind. If the words touched him at all, they were like the rain – striking him with no pain behind their force, sliding down to mix with the mud beneath his feet. He looked down, did a little prance, and noticed that his toes had fused.

He wanted to help this woman, wanted to ease her pain, pass along some comfort, but had no idea how to accomplish this when he didn't understand any longer what she wanted from him. He shivered, wanting to rejoin the warm comfort of the herd. Turning around, he saw that their grazing had taken them across the pasture. Even at this distance, he could pick out the little chestnut mare. Seeing her, he felt his cock stir against his leg.

The woman's scream frightened him. He would have bolted except that the other horses did not. One or two raised their heads with mild equine interest before returning their attention to the ground, so he did likewise, looking over his shoulder. She was pointing at his back and her eyes were enormous.

He contorted his body to look. Dark and light hair grew the length of his neck and halfway down his spine. It wasn't very long yet, perhaps a couple of inches. The down, predominantly white with some black spots, was thicker across his hips and blended to the base of his spine where a tuft of hair, also mixed light and dark and as stiff as a scrub brush, had sprouted. Mild eyes kind, he looked at her. One hand spread against his chest, ruffling the fine hair. "'Far back, far back in our dark soul the horse prances...the symbol of surging potency and power of movement, of action in men.' D.H. Lawrence, *Apocalypse.*" Smiling, glad to be of service, he bobbed his head in farewell, turned and, ignoring her cries, trotted to join his herd.

Darling Wendy

Knife clutched to her chest, Wendy lay in the dark, in her daughter's bed, and waited for the boy.

She knew he'd come, for he'd come every night for the past week. Confident and cocky, arriving swift and silent at the nursery window, he moved with cat-footed assurance along the narrow ledge and perched to listen with an ear to the glass as she read to Jane. The knowledge of his presence was like the brush of silk across Wendy's mind. It had been years, a lifetime, since she'd last felt it.

Her childhood had been spent in this same nursery, with Father stern and distant, and Mother almost cloying in her attempt to make up for her husband's aloof attitude toward his own offspring. Back then, Wendy had shared the room with her brothers – John in the bed nearest hers, sleeping with his knees drawn up to his chin and one of Father's old top hats tipped sideways on the pillow, and Michael beyond him, his round behind prodding the covers into a tent as he snored gustily and drooled onto his teddy bear's head.

She remembered Pan's first appearance, coming then as he did now to listen at the window for stories and songs. Alien, the unaging child was separated from them by more than a thin pane of glass. None of them understood that then, nor would have cared if they had, for he was magic and adventure to the boys... and something else entirely to Wendy, with his lean body striped by shadow and moonlight, and his hair a froth of curls caught up with twigs and leaves that she was forever teasing free.

Their time in Neverland was over too soon, brought about in equal part by Mother's grief and Pan's guilt. Wendy knew that he could have made them stay had he so chosen, and they would have eventually forgotten their earthly home and family. Hurt, she'd wondered why he didn't at least keep her, but when she asked, he refused to say. Still, he came for her the next spring, as promised, missed the following year, then came again. And if what they did in Neverland had little to do with spring cleaning, it was nobody's business but theirs.

After that third spring, when her pregnancy became obvious, she made up a story to protect Pan and withstand Father's rage. Mother remained painfully silent throughout, though with her own secret knowledge, she must have suspected the truth. The Lost Boys' memories of their commander had shredded like mist before the wind of their growing up. Even John and Michael, who surely remembered otherwise, claimed it was only childhood fairy stories and put it down to playing pretend. It was left to Wendy alone to remember fighting pirates, Indian pow-wows, the blaze of starlight across an unobstructed sky, the full moon's lagoon-rippled reflection, mermaid song and, while the boys slept, love in the tall, thick grass.

She was sent away to have the child. When it came, it was a changeling with nut-brown skin, unruly hair, faintly pointed ears, and oddly-hued, sightless eyes. Pan, for all that he'd been born human, was no more human now than his fairy companion. Born dead, the infant was whisked away and disposed of before Wendy had time to do more than hug it once. Two weeks later, she returned home and was ordered – in a heated, private, one-sided conversation with Father – to become a proper young woman. This she dutifully promised to do, all the while secretly waiting for spring and the tap on her window, vowing that this year not even Pan would make her return from Neverland.

He never came. Not that spring, and never again, his short attention span pulling him away, forgetting her in the whirl of other adventures and, so she supposed, other girls as gullible as she. Until now, nearly twenty years later, with her grown, married, and a mother again.

A week ago this very night the hair rose on her neck as she tucked Jane into bed, and she knew with unshakeable certainty that Pan had returned. There was no question that he recognized her as well, and forgot her again in the brief instant his eyes swept past her...and settled on her child.

Despite the balmy nights and Jane's entreaties, the nursery window remained locked. Wendy hardly left her daughter's side at night, her thoughts a roiling mix of a mother's fears spiced with a young girl's jealousy and angry hurt. Each night, seeing him there and pretending she didn't, she drew the curtains closed, barring his curious eyes, and stopped her ears to the *skritch* of fingernails against the glass, telling Jane that it was only tree limbs dancing in the breeze. When her husband (a good man, solid and dependable, nothing at all like Pan) noticed her anxiety and suggested a holiday at the shore, she gratefully agreed and sent her family on ahead, promising to join them after she'd finished some business at home.

Now here she lay, rigid with tension, cramped in the short bed, her fingers tight around the metal shaft between her breasts, graying hair a loose wealth across the pillow, undone like a girl's to make the bait as appealing as possible, knowing that Pan's self-absorption would let him see what he chose to just long enough for her to do what must be done. Old hurts battered her, hardening her resolve. Jane must not be so used, her heart taken and rent, her childhood stolen, her womanhood tainted.

There was no sound to hint that the now unlocked window latch had been tried and lifted, but a change in the air, a scent that was all Neverland, told her that he was in the room even before a flash of light announced Tinkerbelle's presence. Through half-shut eyes, Wendy followed the weave and dart of the tiny, nimble fairy until she settled, quite suddenly, upon an unlit candle stub, where she flickered like a living flame.

"Jane?"

His voice, wild as honey and far-flung mint, caressed her, raising gooseflesh, lighting her from within like hot gold in her veins, warming her thighs despite her promise that things would be different for Jane.

For *her*.

"Jane?"

Closer now. She imagined the liquid touch of his hand on the coverlet over her feet, but did not raise her head to see. The girl's desire betrayed the woman's rage, making her ache for him even as she tightened her grip on the knife.

"Jane." An edge of command, less the captain ordering his troop of boys than the petulant child, tired of waiting for his treat. "Wake up, Jane."

The whisper of bare feet on carpet and the sudden near smell of *newleavesdewstarlightocean darkearthmagic* made her squeeze her eyes shut as his hand fit along the curve of her shoulder with gentle familiarity. "Don't be frightened. I have a surprise for you."

She sat up fast and swept the bedclothes aside as she jabbed with the knife. Pan, quicker than she remembered, danced out of the way and was suddenly airborne and well out of reach of her frenzied, leaping thrusts. His shadow, reattached so long ago, bobbed against the ceiling in time to the Tink-candle's pulsing flash.

"Wendy!" He was all admonishment, hovering several feet above her head. "Put that down! You almost cut me!"

Bitter laughter galled her throat. "I'll do more than cut you!"

"But why?" he asked, perplexed.

"You know why!"

For an instant, the look in Pan's eyes shifted. Anyone else would have missed it. But Wendy glimpsed the feral child behind the playful boy; saw the wild thing, lips bloodied, that peered from the too-knowing depths of his eyes. Then his narrow shoulders shrugged in their tunic of thin deer hide and the creature was gone, leaving the boy behind.

"Is this one of your games? It seems very silly." His tone was cavalier, dismissing her as he always had. "I've come to get you for spring cleaning." He said it like it was the simplest thing in the world. Perhaps, to him, it was. "Are you ready?" Hovering lower, he held out his hand.

She stared at it, studying the lean line of bone and sinew beneath sun-baked skin. The lines of his palm were encrusted with something dark, soil from digging or blood from the hunt. An odor lifted from it, heady as wine. How long had she waited to hear those words? How many springs had she lain awake, night after tearful night, waiting for a Pan who never came, wanting him, afraid with a desperate certainty that some other Wendy-bird flew his skies in her place?

His fingers wiggled impatiently. "Come on, Wendy!"

Sighing, a tiny sobbing breath adrift in the expanse of time lost, she reached and took his hand. For a moment there was compliance, and then her fingers slid up over his child-sized fist to latch firmly around his slender wrist. Pan hauled back in surprise, jerking to break free, but she had him now and twisted the arm sideways until he cried with pain. Old she might be, and a mere female in his eyes, but she'd been taught to fight by none other than Peter Pan himself, taught tactics to keep pirates at bay, never dreaming they'd be used on him.

He kicked her on the side of the head so hard that her vision dimmed. In the narrow shaft of sight, she watched him grasp the dagger at his waist and jerk it free.

The room blazed with light, banishing shadows in a bath of brilliance that lit even the farthest corners. Tink, always Wendy's enemy, burned with fire, her tiny form the center of a blazing aureole that hurt the eyes. Launching from her candle throne, Pan's fairy shot toward the ceiling, spun, and plummeted like a falling sun.

She hit him square in the back, forcing him onto Wendy's blade. It vanished like a magician's sword, buried to the hilt in his old-young flesh, and Wendy's fist was hot with sudden blood. Pan collapsed, curling into himself, and dropped from the air, driving her to the floor. Warmth soaked her nightgown as the hot musk of the hunt filled her nose.

The long ends of her hair tainted with his blood, Wendy struggled from beneath him. Devoid of pain, his terribly lucid eyes stared into hers as he daubed fitfully at his chest, raising his fingers to gaze at the smear of red. "I can't die," he whispered plaintively, as if to argue the point.

On her knees, Wendy backed away from him, her hands leaving bloody prints on the ruined carpet. Shakily, she rose and stood over him.

Something surfaced in his eyes. Where before it had been vulpine and maybe more than a little rabid, now she saw what was, perhaps, the true Pan, the child who'd first run away from his pram, the thoughtless beast who, with no more intent to do harm or understanding of it than a kitten, had inflicted nothing else his entire life.

"Tink..." His last breath was the sough of wind through leaves. His hand curled against his chest and he was gone.

The peal of tiny bells filled the room, and it took Wendy a moment to realize that it was the sound of fairy laughter, triumphant and vindicated. Looking up, she found Tinkerbelle poised on the mantle, legs spread, fists on hips. For the first time, their eyes met with understanding, then Tink gifted her with a grim nod and launched herself through the open window.

The damp folds of her nightgown twisting around her bare legs, Wendy followed, pushing the casement farther open to stare at the sky. In the distance, a tiny light pulsed once and then vanished amid the wealth of stars.

Eyes sweeping the heavens, she found what she sought without much effort, for she'd never lost sight of it, even in growing up. And she knew that she no longer needed Pan, or Tink's pixie dust, to get there. Lifting her gown above her knees, she stepped onto the window seat and from there to the ledge, her toes curling against the sill as she paused for a moment. Then, arms wide, the Wendy-bird took flight.